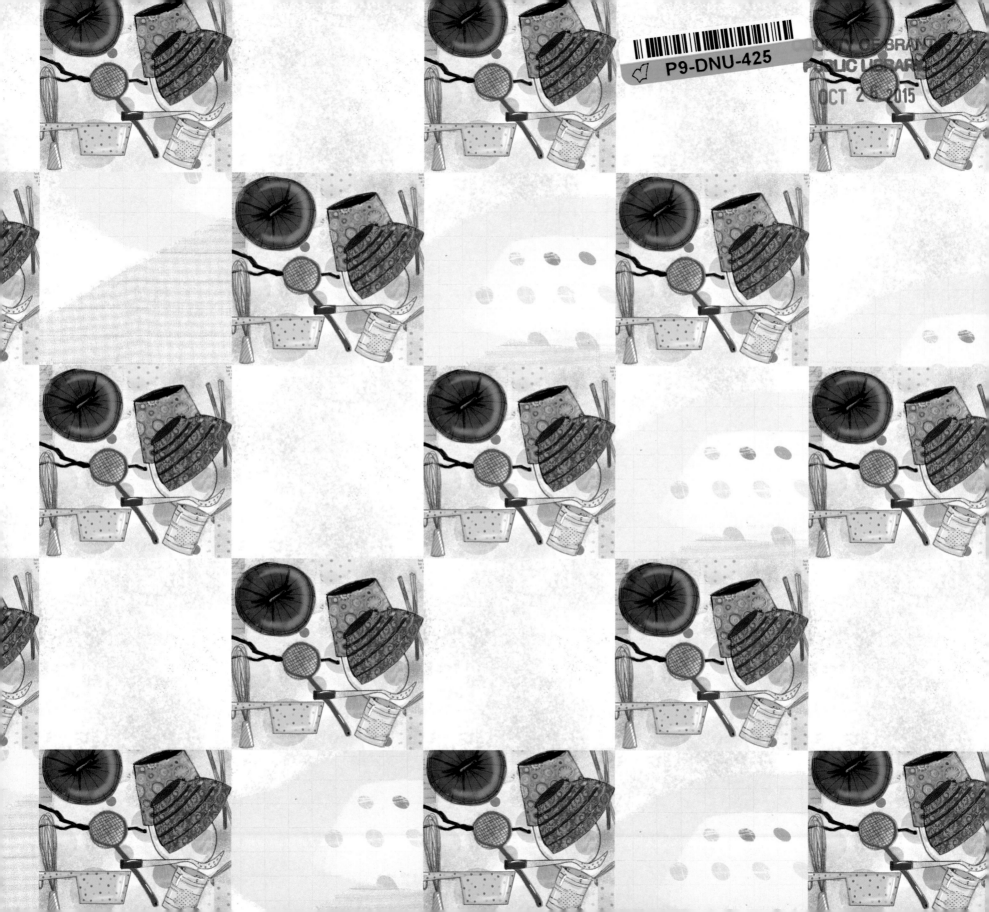

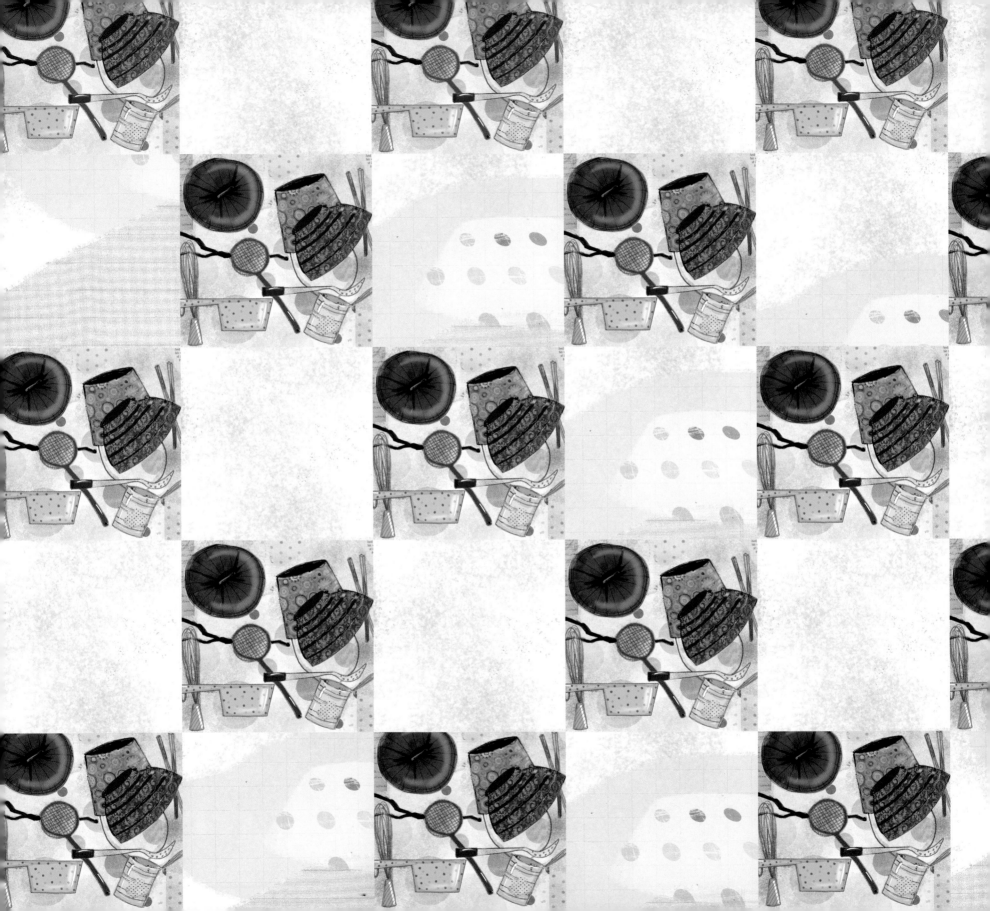

Drum City

Drum City

by **Thea Guidone**

Illustrations by **Vanessa Newton**

Dragonfly Books ⸺🪰 New York

Drum.
Drum.

Boy in the yard
drumming so **hard**,

calling all kids
to come drum in the yard.

Drum on some kettles and cans!

Here they come!

They run to the beat of the **drum**.

Drum.

Bowls and **buckets,**

cartons and cans,

barrels and bins,

and pots and pans,

mops on pails,

and **rusty** old rails—

a frolicking, rollicking ruckus of rumbling **drums**.

Drum.

Jump to the sound,
  dance all around,

loud on the tubs and the
  tins that they found.

"**March!**" calls the boy
  in the yard full of drums,

hundreds and
  hundreds of
    drums.

Hum of the city.

Humdrum of the city. HO-hum.

Something is coming.

They watch and they wonder,

assuming the booming

is summertime thunder.

Thumping and **pounding,**

the echo resounding

the sound of the

pound of the **drums.**

Drum.

Buses and cabs,

bakers and cops,

people in **banks,**

people in shops,

everywhere, everything, everyone

STOPS

for **kids** marching in
with their
drums.

Drum.

People in traffic keeping the beat
on the **hood** and the trunk
and the bicycle seat.

Mamas in rollers
rock babies in strollers,

clapping and **stomp**ing and
stamping their feet to the

drums.

Drum.

Drums everywhere,
in the park, in the square,

by the **pond** with the ducks,
in the zoo with the **bear**.

From Hill Street to **Main**
to Sassafras Lane,

kids **shake** up
the **city** with

drums.

IN-SPIRE', v. i. [-ED; -ING.] [Lat.
inspirare.] To inhale air into the
lungs. —v. t. 1. To breathe into.
2. To infuse by breathing. 3. To
affect, as with a supernatural influ-
ence. 4. To inhale.

Drum.

The **city** becomes a city of **drums**,

banging and clanging as **everyone** comes.

A **summer** parade, a drummer parade,

a magical bucket-and-bowl

serenade

Drum.

Up in the **planes**,
down at the docks,

bang on a lid or a crate
or a **box**.

Everyone jams.
Everyone
rocks.

Everyone,
beat on your
drum.

Drum.

Play **hard**, play soft,
  play happy or **blue**.

You listen to **me**.
  I listen to **you**.

Over the mountains
and over the **sea**,

drumming like you,
drumming like me.

Together we **drum**.

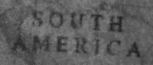

Let's

drum!

For kids in my family and kids in "The Group."
—T.G.

This is dedicated to my sister, my friend,
my 20/20 and my hilariously funny family.
Thank you JC, Ray, Coy, Will, Zoe, Ben, Chyna,
The Jeans, Loredan, Ms. I, and Dad.
Love y'all.
—V.N.

Text copyright © 2010 by Thea Guidone
Cover art and interior illustrations copyright © 2010 by Vanessa Newton
Design by Becky James

Visit us on the Web! randomhousekids.com

Educators and librarians, for a variety of teaching tools, visit us at RHTeachersLibrarians.com

The Library of Congress has cataloged the hardcover edition of this work as follows:
Guidone, Thea.
Drum city / by Thea Guidone; illustrations by Vanessa Newton. — 1st ed.
p. cm.
Summary: A young boy begins banging on pots and pans in his front yard, enticing other children to join
him, and before long the entire city is feeling the beat.
[1. Stories in rhyme. 2. Drum—Fiction.] I. Newton, Vanessa, ill. II. Title.
PZ8.3.G948Dru 2010 [E]—dc22 2009031747

ISBN 978-1-58246-308-7 (trade) — ISBN 978-1-58246-348-3 (lib. bdg.) —
ISBN 978-0-553-52350-8 (pbk.) — ISBN 978-0-385-38730-9 (ebook)

MANUFACTURED IN CHINA
10 9 8 7 6 5 4 3 2 1
First Dragonfly Books Edition